11/11/23 50p

HTH

D1313302

Get **more** out of libraries

Please return or renew this item by the last date shown.

You can renew online at www.hants.gov.uk/library

Or by phoning 0300 555 1387

Hampshire
County Council

C016089364

Books About Bonnie:

Best Dog Bonnie

BEL MOONEY

Illustrated by Sarah McMenemy

WALKER BOOKS

First published 2008 by Walker Books Ltd
87 Vauxhall Walk, London SE11 5HJ

This edition published 2013

2 4 6 8 10 9 7 5 3 1

Text © 2008 Bel Mooney
Illustrations © 2008 Sarah McMenemy

The right of Bel Mooney and Sarah McMenemy to be identified as
author and illustrator respectively of this work has been asserted by
them in accordance with the Copyright, Designs and Patents Act 1988

This book has been typeset in StempelSchneidler

Printed and bound in Great Britain by Clays Ltd, St Ives plc.

British Library Cataloguing in Publication Data:
a catalogue record for this book is available from the British Library

ISBN 978-1-4063-5098-2

www.walker.co.uk

For Gaynor and Lily
B.M.

To my grandmother, Jean,
who had a Bonnie dog
S.M.

⁕ OK ⁕

"She's looking very scruffy, Harry," said
Mum, as Bonnie scuttled across the living-
room floor after the ball.

"I like her scruffy," said Harry.

They hadn't had the little dog very long,
but she was certainly looking very grubby
indeed. Her white coat was turning grey,
the ends of her ears had dabbled in her
dinner, and there were
black stains streaking
down from her eyes.

7

Because they'd never had a dog before, they didn't quite know how to look after her.

"Can't you just turn the hose on her?" joked Zack, Harry's friend from next door.

"Can I brush her?" asked his twin sister Zena, picking Bonnie up.

Harry handed her the dog brush, but Bonnie wriggled like an eel and Zena soon gave up – just like Harry did, when he remembered to try, which wasn't often.

"Raggy rabbit," teased Zena.

"Messy mouse," said Harry.

"Pongy puppy," laughed Zack.

"I felt all these knots in her coat," Zena said, frowning. "But if you tug at them she'll yelp. What are you going to do, Harry?"

Harry didn't know. His dream pet had been a huge dog called Prince, with a short, shiny black and brown mixed coat, and sharp ears that pricked up when he came into the room. But Mum had got them quite the opposite, and although Harry liked Bonnie now, he could see she was a lot of trouble to take care of. I mean – a white dog? One game of footie and she'd have to go in the washing machine!

"Yes, pets need a lot of care," said Harry's mother, "and we need to find out more."

They went to the library, but there were no books on small white dogs. Next stop was the pet shop, where there were guides to Labradors, collies, cats and goldfish, but nothing about posh Maltese dogs.

"Let me look it up on the computer," said the shop assistant, and she clicked away until a big smile spread across her face. "There's a book called *The Maltese Today*. Would you like me to order it for you? It'll be here in a couple of days."

Then she peered over the counter and frowned at Bonnie. "She needs a bath!"

So they bought dog shampoo, conditioner to detangle her coat, eye-stain wipes and her own sponge, and went home to give Bonnie her first bath. Of course, Zack and Zena came round as well.

Harry was quite excited – but as soon as Bonnie saw them running the water she fled.

"She understands," laughed Harry, "and she doesn't like baths!"

Black eyes gleamed from beneath his bed, bright as buttons. Harry reached under and gently pulled her out. "You have to get clean, Mouse-Face," he whispered. "I don't always like baths myself!"

He carried her to the bathroom. Bonnie began to shiver and shake until Zena couldn't bear it. "Oh, she's really scared!"

"She thinks she'll go down the plughole," said Zack.

"In you go," Harry said, holding her over the bath.

If Bonnie could have flown she would have been out of there, but there was no escape. She was lowered into the warm soapy water before you could say "small grey dog", and then Mum sponged more water over her head.

Harry began to laugh. He couldn't help it. Bonnie looked so funny, her thick coat soaking wet and flattened to nothing, which showed how tiny she was underneath. The hair on her curly tail hung like shreds and he could see pink mottled skin beneath the wet fur.

She wasn't a pretty sight.

"Mmm," grinned Zack. "The words *drowned* and *rat* come to mind!"

"Mean!" giggled Zena.

11

"Come on, gang, we have to take this seriously," ordered Harry's mum.

"We'll take an end each," Harry decided. "I'll wash her head and shoulders and front paws. You do her ... other end."

"Thanks," muttered Mum.

It was soon over. They wrapped the squirming Bonnie in a towel and the laughter began again. Her little face poked out just like ET, a creature from another world longing to get back into its spaceship and escape. Be anywhere but here.

Harry's mum gave Zena the hairdryer – and then the trouble *really* began. Bonnie hated being dried. The more they did it, the wilder her coat became, and by the time Mum came back in from the kitchen Bonnie looked like a mad snowball. And Zack had twisted the hair on top of her head into punk icicle spikes.

All three children burst out laughing at Mum's face. Bonnie certainly looked cleaner – but she was still far from the pretty white dog Harry's mother had rescued from the RSPCA home.

"Right!" said Mum. "Stand aside. I'm officially taking over this dog beauty business."

Uh-oh, thought Harry.

Two days later, Mum collected the book from the pet shop, and there on the front cover was a Maltese – a real princess of a dog. She had long ears down to her knees, a dazzling white coat, long and silky, and a little pink bow on top of her head, gathering up the long hair so it didn't fall into her eyes. The show Maltese stared out from the book as if she knew she was beautiful, as if there wasn't an animal in the world she'd be afraid of.

"Oh, how *lovely*!" breathed Mum.

"Yuck," snapped Harry. "I'd hate our Bons to be a prissy mutt like that."

But he was worried by the glint in his mother's eye.

The same day, Mum found a dog grooming salon called Millionhairs, and they had a spare appointment. Harry didn't understand how Bonnie knew, but as soon as Mum opened the car door she dived off his lap and tried to hide under the seat. Mum scooped her up, and she started that terrified shaking again.

"D-d-don't l-l-leave me, Harry," she seemed to be saying.

The young woman in the salon frowned at the clean-but-tangled Bonnie, told them you had to groom dogs *before* you bathed them – and promised to put everything right.

"Are you trying to grow her hair?" she asked.

Mum pulled the new book
out of her shopping bag. "Well, how
long would it take for her to look like *that*?"
Harry was sure Bonnie was asking him to
get her out of there. Her black eyes *begged*
to be rescued. But there was nothing he
could do. Not once Mum had made her
mind up about something. She'd been so
cheerful lately, and he knew it was because

of the dog and their friendly new neighbours – and the fact that she was getting used to Dad not being around. So he didn't want to spoil her fun. But he didn't want his fun with Bonnie spoiled either.

When they got home the flat felt very empty. Harry wandered into their garden and called over the fence for Zack and Zena, but they weren't around. He watched some TV but there was nothing good on. He felt cross and restless – and Mum noticed.

"Admit it, Harry, you really love Bonnie now!" she said, with that annoying smile people have when they know they've won an argument.

"Uh, she's OK," Harry mumbled.

It shocked him to realize how much he missed the small white dog who had come into his life so unexpectedly. Worse, he dreaded what she would look like when she came home. It was bad enough having

a girly dog, without her looking like
something a model might tuck under her
arm to go shopping. How would he ever
live it down?

Help! thought Harry. And inside his head
he seemed to hear a little answering yelp.

Two hours later, the phone rang. It was time
to collect Bonnie from Millionhairs.

Mum went into the salon and came out
five minutes later holding a beautiful
little toy – so pure white and fluffy
she might have been taken out of
a box on Christmas Day.
Her tail waved
like a silk flag,
and – horror
of horrors – she
wore a tiny pink
bow on one side
of her head.

When Mum put her in the car Bonnie jumped all over Harry, licking him and yelping with joy at being back with the people she loved. Despite himself, Harry laughed, cowering under her kisses.

"Look at you!" he said. "Get the pink bow!"

"So sweet – and she smells like flowers," cooed Mum.

"Can I take it out right now?" asked Harry.

"No, you cannot!" said Mum "Don't you think she looks gorgeous?"

Now, the truth was, Harry *did* think Bonnie looked cute, but he didn't want to admit it. In his mind he was the big, tough boy who raced around the park with his big, tough dog at his heels, so that no Mean People would ever dare say anything bad to them for fear of those great yellow fangs and that blood-shivering growl. But in his

heart he knew he was just little Harry who
loved Bonnie, the smallest dog in the world
— who was now officially the prettiest
dog in the country, and who always
made girls and old ladies
say *"Aaaah!"*

In his dreams
Harry and his hound would
be joined in the park by Dad, and they'd
all play football. Dad would say how fast
Harry was getting, and he'd have biscuits in
his pocket for Prince, and it'd be brilliant.

In reality Harry hadn't seen his father for five weeks, and lived in a flat with his mum and a minuscule mutt with a pink bow in her hair.

What could you do?

Harry stroked Bonnie as Mum drove home, entwining his fingertips in the softness of her squeaky-clean ears. Keep your dreams to yourself and make the best of what you've got, he told himself.

When they got home Mum sat down at the living-room table and started to read the book about Maltese dogs.

"I didn't realize it's such an old breed," she called out. "It says here the Chinese emperors had dogs just like Bonnie…"

"Yeah, carried around on a silk cushion by a slave," muttered Harry from the sofa.

After a while Mum grabbed the remote and switched the TV off, her face all lit up.

"Listen, sweetheart, I've just had the best idea ever!"

"Ye–es?" said Harry warily.

"You know you're always saying I need to find myself a hobby so I won't get a bit sad, like I sometimes do?"

"Ye–es," said Harry again.

"Well, this is what I'm going to do: make myself a real Maltese expert – and turn Bonnie into a champion dog! There's a dog show in town in a couple of months, and she could win a rosette. She might even win Best in Show! And after that – Crufts! Then we could get her a boyfriend, have puppies, who knows? Oh, I'm *so* excited!"

Harry's heart dropped into his trainers. But his mum's face shone, and she clutched Bonnie so close that their faces squashed together and the dog appeared to be smiling.

"Don't you agree, love?"

Harry groaned inside. He knew "OK" was the only possible reply.

Bonnie liked feeling clean.
The only thing wrong was something caught in her hair above her right eye which pulled a bit. But never mind — it was good to be home. She'd been afraid when her pack left her in that noisy place with the sprays, the hairdryers and the other dogs looking as miserable as she felt.

That old West Highland terrier told her all he wanted was to turn into a Scottie. When Bonnie asked why, he looked at her as if saying "Duh!" Then Bonnie got it: a black Scottie doesn't show the dirt.

The brushing hurt, the water got in her eyes, the hairdryer roared in her ears ... but here she was, nestled on the sofa between Harry and Mum — clean. She liked it when they made nice sounds at her, and being clean seemed to bring more nice sounds than usual. And they were talking about her, a lot.

But like all dogs, Bonnie had a good deal of magic in her. She knew what Harry was feeling even before he did. So why wasn't he happy, even though he was smiling at his mum?

Bonnie rolled over on her side and stretched. I'll find out.

❖ GOOD ❖

Harry and his mum took Bonnie for a walk in the park. They didn't do it very often; her legs were so short Mum said that taking her to the end of their road and back was enough.

"That's cos you're lazy, Mum!" Harry joked.

But it was a sunny Saturday and Harry suspected Mum wanted to show off their pet's newly acquired model good looks. Bonnie played the part perfectly, prancing along on her black velvet lead with her head high and her tail curled over her back. Every few steps they were stopped by some elderly lady who would fix soppy eyes on Bonnie and coo, "Oh, who's a good little dog then?"

And: "Aren't you *beautiful*?"

And: "I've never seen such a *sweet* little animal!"

Harry scowled. "Why do they call her a good dog when they don't know her?"

26

"It's because she looks so adorable," said Mum.

"But that's stupid! Just because you *look* sweet doesn't mean you *are* sweet!"

"In Bonnie's case it does."

"Not really. She could be a vicious cat-killer for all they know!"

Just then another lady came up. She had
wild grey hair and wore little purple glasses
that matched her long patchwork skirt.
When she bent down to pat Bonnie, four big
silver bracelets crashed down her wrist,
making the dog jump. She was really quite
old but she didn't dress old, and when she
smiled at Harry, her eyes wrinkled up
so much he couldn't help
but like her.

"I love your dog! What kind is she?"

"A Maltese," answered Mum.

"Is she a puppy?"

"No," said Harry, "this is as big as she gets."

"Never mind," said the old lady. "Good things come in small parcels."

That reminded Harry of what his dad used to say when Harry moaned that he was smaller than all the other boys in his class. Remembering made him itchy and cross.

"Not always," he snapped. "I mean, if you were given a new sports car it'd be a pretty big parcel. And a poisonous spider in a box would be tiny, wouldn't it?"

Bonnie looked up at him, as if to ask what was wrong, and her tail drooped a little. That made him feel itchier than ever. Why couldn't he just be nice to everybody, even old ladies in the park?

"Hmm, I follow your thinking, young man," she replied. "Don't judge anything by its packaging, eh? Especially small dogs and young boys – and old ladies too, I reckon!" She whispered the last part to Harry, and shot him a cheeky wink. "By the way, my name's Olga," she said, holding out her hand to Mum. "I come here every day, so maybe we'll bump into each other again."

Harry's mother was quiet until they reached the car, and then she said, "I don't know what's got into you, Harry! Why are you such a grouch today?"

Bonnie snuggled onto his knee, a round white ball of fluff with her pink tongue sticking out like a rose petal. He knew that if she'd been a cat she'd have purred. The thought of Bonnie purring made him smile, and when he smiled her tail waved like a flag. The more he smiled the more she waved.

"Wag, wag, wag," he said.

"That's better," Mum called over her shoulder as she drove.

But after lunch Harry's good mood disappeared once more. "I'm going round to Zack and Zena's to see if we can muck about in their sandpit," he announced.

"You are not," said Mum. "It's time for Bonnie's grooming. If we don't get into the habit she'll get all messy again – and I don't want her coming back covered in sand."

She marched into the kitchen to fetch what she insisted on calling Bonnie's Beauty Bag and Harry flopped down on the sofa in despair. Bonnie did her brilliant helicopter take-off to leap up beside him. She gave a little shiver and looked at him with those pleading eyes.

"I'm sorry, girl, but it's too late to stop her now. You know what Mum's like once she's on a mission…"

31

Bonnie put her head on one side as if to say, "Well?"

"She's got her heart set on this dog show business, you know?"

Bonnie flopped her head down on her outstretched paws and closed her eyes. What could they do?

Mum spread a towel out on the floor; with a brush in one hand and a metal comb in the other she looked like a cook about to carve a turkey.

That's what
Bonnie thought
anyway, because
she was off that sofa
and under the kitchen
table before Harry
could blink.

"Go and get her,
please," ordered Mum
in that voice which
said, "I get *so* tired trying
to do my best for this boy and this dog."

But Bonnie didn't want to be *got*. She ran
round the kitchen four times with Harry
chasing her, then into his room and under
the bed. When he tried to pull her out, she
darted through to the other side, and tore
past him into Mum's room.

Harry started to laugh. "Racing dog!"
he spluttered.

"Hurry *up*, Harry!" called Mum.

Harry had no choice: he scooped Bonnie up and carried her wriggling to the towel. There she sank her tiny teeth into the beauty bag and shook it to and fro like a terrier killing a rat – scattering scissors, cotton buds, toothbrush and dog toothpaste everywhere.

"Mrrrer … mrrrer," she growled.

"Bonnie! You naughty dog!" cried Mum, while Harry tried to stifle his giggles.

He grabbed the brush and started attacking Bonnie's waving tail with such speed that she was too surprised to squirm.

Soon the job was done, and Bonnie's coat was silkier than ever. But Mum hadn't finished. She took out a tape measure.

"What's that for?"

"I want to see how long her ears are. The longer they grow, the more she'll look like the dog on the book cover, like a proper show Maltese. And then she might win a silver cup!"

Harry groaned. A silver cup? This was getting serious.

A few days later, Mum announced that she had a new routine. Every day, when Harry was in school, she took Bonnie to the park.

"We both need the exercise," she said, then added, "and anyway … it's nice to chat to people."

"What people?"

"People Bonnie introduces me to, of course!"

Harry could see such a difference in his mum. It was as if she'd taken off a grey coat and put on a pink one, and its colour showed in her cheeks. She called Bonnie "my best friend", and made such a fuss of her all the time that Harry almost felt jealous. But did he want all his mum's attention or the dog's? He wasn't sure.

"Why's life so complicated, Bons?" he whispered as she cuddled up to him watching TV.

In reply, Bonnie licked his fingers enthusiastically – as if they tasted of chicken and chocolate all mixed up. As if she was saying that even complicated, mixed-up feelings could be good.

The Friday after that walk in the park, Harry strolled to the school gate with a wonderful, happy, end-of-the-week feeling. School had been good: he had loads of friends now and didn't feel like the new kid any more, and the boys had stopped teasing him for being small. One of the girls in his class brushed past him going in the opposite direction because she'd forgotten something.

"I just saw your mum, Harry, with that cute little dog of yours."

"Hers," said Harry.

"Whatever. She's got somebody with her as well."

Harry started to ask who, but the girl had rushed on.

A little flame of excitement sparked like a match in his chest. Dad! It must be his dad – who else would come to the school to meet him? Maybe that's why Mum had been looking so cheerful. Dad had come to see them!

He started to walk very quickly, then trot. But when he raced out of the school gate, disappointment flared red in his face.

Bonnie was rearing on her hind legs, pulling on the lead and yelping like she always did when she saw him. But his mum was standing next to a lady with wild grey hair, a purple skirt, big silver earrings and a long woolly cardigan.

Mum was beaming. "Do you remember Olga? She's my and Bonnie's new friend, Harry – and she's coming home to tea."

"Guess what?" said Olga. "Bonnie recognized me, and ran towards me barking her head off. So we reckon she wants us all to be friends."

Harry managed a tight grin. "Good old Bons," he mumbled.

BONNIE looked with disgust at her plate of healthy-all-in-one-veterinary-diet-dental-care biscuits. Was she really supposed to eat this? Where was that squishy chicken stuff out of the tin?

Or the turkey with vegetables from
the little tray with the peel-back lid?

Was this how she was rewarded for looking after
them? For introducing them to Mum's new friend,
the old lady whose hair needed grooming? Did
they think this was the way to treat a proud and
hungry dog who spent her life cheering Harry up?

It was all the fault of that book Mum kept
reading. Oh yes, she knew. The dry food was
so her ears wouldn't get dirty. And there it was on
the plate. A pile of brown pellets just like the ones
at the bottom of Zack and Zena's rabbit's cage.

Yuck, thought Bonnie. Something will have
to be done. At the right moment.

Better

Harry didn't know what to do.
Mum was getting worse.
She was driving him mad.
She brushed Bonnie every day,
crooning, "Come to Mummy"
and "Who's Mummy's precious
baby?" and "Mummy knows
it hurts when there's a tangle" – and icky
things like that.

Sometimes Harry caught Bonnie looking
at him as if to plead, "Get me out of here!"

Soon it all merged in his mind into one long "Oogly-woogly-babbie-Mummy-brushy-wushy-moodly-*moo*."

Yuck. *Double yuck.*

"It's all right to love your dog," he told Zack and Zena. "I mean, I love Bonnie myself. But Mum's obsessed! It's ever since she got this nutty idea about the dog show."

"What if Bonnie doesn't win anything?" asked Zena.

"Don't even think about it," said Harry, looking gloomy.

"She needs distracting," said Zack.

"What with? I thought it was good when she said she had a new hobby," said Harry, "but now she's got to have the best Maltese in town and get on the telly!

It's all she thinks about. She never goes out, except to take Bonnie to the park."

They were all lolling about in the Wilsons' big sitting room, feeling lazy. Harry loved this room; in fact he loved their neighbours' whole house. It was full of great things to look at – glittering mineral rocks piled in bowls, a stone Buddha, giant cushions embroidered with mirrors, glowing rugs on polished floors, and pictures and books everywhere.

Harry felt guilty for preferring it to their own small flat. In his heart he thought it was all his dad's fault, for causing them to move, for not being there any more ... yet he didn't want to think that. He hated feeling cross with Dad, but the crossness was real and sat like a stone in the middle of his chest. Sometimes he looked at Bonnie and thought how easy it must be to be a dog. So uncomplicated.

He reached out and stroked Bonnie's ears, which were long and silky now. "Don't have a worry in the world, do you, Bons?" He smiled. "I wish I was a dog."

"Your mum'd have you sraight down Millionhairs!" said Zack.

"Groom Harry!" laughed Zena, ruffling his hair. "Grow his ears!"

Bonnie fixed her coal-black eyes on Harry and snuffled his hand. Then she rolled over, putting her front paws over her eyes and

making odd little
yelping sounds,
which was a sign
she wanted to play.
Rolling back, she crouched
down. She stamped one
front paw after the other,
growling, and made little runs at Harry,
until he was weak with laughter.

They all leaped up and played "chase
Bonnie around the room and capture her",
which took a long time because there were
so many places to hide and Bonnie moved
so quickly on those short, furry legs.

At last they trapped her in a corner
and she reared up on her hind
legs and did a dance, front
paws in the air. Laughing,
Harry gathered her up in
his arms and planted a kiss
on the top of her head.

"I'm glad you're not too posh to play,"
he whispered.

The three of them went into the Wilsons'
shiny kitchen, Zack found apple juice and
chocolate biscuits, and they sat down
at the table to talk.

"So, what are we going to do
about your mum?" asked Zack.

Harry shrugged. "Dunno.
Might help if she went out
more. On her own, I mean."

Just then Mrs Wilson
swept into the room.

The twins' mum was
different from Harry's:
Rosie Wilson had
long curly red hair and
wore jeans and trendy
T-shirts and trainers,
or flowing skirts and
high-heeled boots.

She never looked tired or sad; her mouth turned up at the corners. Mr Wilson was just the same. He worked at home, in a big room at the top of the house. Zena and Zack saw a lot of their dad. They were lucky.

"I've got an idea!" Zena burst out.

"Mu–um?"

"Hmm?"

"What about that jazz thing on Saturday? Can Harry's mum go with you? Can she? Harry and Bonnie could come round here. *Please*, Mum."

Harry frowned. "I dunno – she'll say she hasn't got anything to wear. Anyway, she'd need a ticket, wouldn't she?"

"No, we've got a spare," said Mrs Wilson.

"You *have* to persuade her, Harry," said Zena. "She'll have a great time, and so will we! It'll make her feel better."

"Better than what?" asked Zack.

"Just better," said his mum, with that mischievous smile Harry liked so much. "I'll give her a ring."

Mum came off the phone. As Harry expected, she'd said no to the invitation – and given the reason that she didn't like leaving Bonnie and Harry, because Harry wouldn't want to be left with a strange babysitter. It was rubbish, and they both knew it. The truth was, she was frightened and shy, and lots of other things too.

But Harry was determined to do something.

Next day, on the way to school, he asked if Mum was meeting Olga in the park that afternoon.

"Yes, I always run into her. She's so nice."

"Will you bring her to meet me? I'd like to see her again."

"All right, love, I will. I think she gets a bit lonely, so she'll be pleased to see you."

When Harry picked Bonnie up to say goodbye he whispered, "Stage one of the plan, Mouse-Face."

Today Olga was wearing a green shawl over a cream linen skirt, and her long beads and earrings were the colour of new leaves. Her hair was still a bit mad but she looked cool

for an old lady, and Harry found himself
thinking what a good granny she'd make.

He didn't waste time.

"Olga – if Mum went out on Saturday
night, would you come round to ours and be
babysitter for me and Bonnie?"

His mother started to shake her head,
but Olga didn't notice. "I can't think of
anything I'd like better!"
she cried.

"Oh, thanks for asking me, Harry! What fun… This has made my week!"

What could Harry's mum say after that? When she complained she had nothing to wear, Olga got bossy. "But there's that nice pink jacket – brightest thing you've got, my girl. And why not treat yourself to something new?"

As they walked ahead talking (at least, Olga talked and Mum looked worried), Harry bent down to Bonnie and whispered, "Mission accomplished."

Later he slipped next door with Bonnie and told Zack and Zena the good news. Mrs Wilson ruffled his hair and said, "You can all stay here, and I'll get some food for the four of you."

"And we can play on the PlayStation, Haz!" said Zack.

Harry went pink. He liked his new nickname – it sounded cool – and he liked the idea of Saturday night at the Wilsons' with Olga; but most of all he loved the thought of his mum going out and having fun. Seeing him smile, Bonnie leaped up onto his lap and started to lick his face like mad.

"She thinks you need a wash, Haz!" said Zack.

Next day, outside school, Mum had Bonnie's lead in one hand and two carrier bags in the other.

"I thought I'd see what I could get for Saturday night," she explained, "and in the end I found this gorgeous black dress in the Oxfam shop. I hope it's the right kind of thing. Then I saw these shoes in a sale, and ... well, it's taken me so long I haven't had time to groom Bonnie!"

"Oh, she looks fine to me," said Harry casually.

Saturday came. Harry's mum was excited and nervous at the same time, and once again Bonnie's grooming session was neglected.

"You've got to groom yourself, Mum!" said Harry. She fussed over her hair ("Looks nice when you fluff it up," said Harry), whether she should wear make-up ("Yes"), and whether people would know the dress was second-hand ("Not if you take the tag off it!").

By the time Olga arrived carrying a large shopping bag, Harry felt quite proud of his mum. In her black dress and pointy high heels she looked just as glamorous as Mrs Wilson.

When they trooped next door, Mr Wilson gave her a wolf whistle that made them all laugh, and she blushed as pink as her jacket.

Once the parents had left, and before anybody could grab the TV remote, Olga told them she was an artist and that was why she'd brought along paper, pastels and pencils – because they were all going to have a go at painting. Zack looked longingly in the direction of the PlayStation, but he didn't know Olga well enough to protest.

"So what do we do?" asked Harry.

"We're going to find one thing to draw, and then paint it in lots of different styles, as crazy as you like, so we can have an art exhibition for your parents when they get back," said Olga. "You can try and make it look lifelike, but then do it as an abstract too. And what about lots of little dots? Look – I've brought a book to show you."

They gathered round as she turned
the pages, telling them the names of the
different styles and artists, and encouraged
them to go wild with their pictures.

"But what are we going to paint, Olga?"
asked Harry.

"Can't you guess?"
And she swooped
down and carried
Bonnie to the table.
Bonnie sat still
while they drew her,
then curled up in a ball for another pose, then
ran around the room because Olga said all
artists had to learn how
to draw quickly. Harry
couldn't stop laughing
at Zack's abstract,
which made Bonnie
look like a collection
of white cottages;

and at Zena's dot painting,
which made her look like
she had measles.

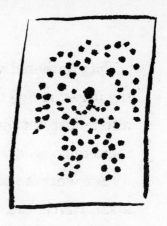

Zack stared at Harry's
drawings. "You're better
than us, Haz," he said.

"Good, better, best –
what does it matter?"
asked Olga. "You've all
done Bonnie proud, and
that's what counts."

They ate jacket potatoes,
cold chicken and salad, and
Bonnie was rewarded for her
patience when Harry chopped up a delicious
piece of meat for her. Olga sipped a glass of
white wine and told them stories about
when she was young and lived in Russia,
and painted pictures with household
paint because she couldn't buy
the real thing.

They drew some more, then put the pictures up on the wall with Blu-Tack and before they knew it they heard a key in the lock.

Harry hadn't seen his mum look so happy since … well, since things with Dad started to go wrong. There was a lot of laughter in the air, and even more when they looked at the drawings.

As Harry cuddled Bonnie until she could hardly breathe, everybody agreed that his picture of her in the style of Picasso was great, even though Bonnie had three eyes. Harry looked around at their new friends and felt, for the first time, that things were definitely *better*.

BONNIE chewed at one of her claws.

She stretched, listening to Harry's breathing.

He and his mum had both looked happy tonight,

and so something in Bonnie's heart relaxed.

She felt pleased with herself; it was all part of

her plan. And it was worth all the fuss and the

white paint splashing about and seeing them

turn her into the weirdest things ... to munch

on real chicken, for a change.

She closed her eyes. A radiator made a

gurgling noise in the darkness, and she scanned

the room, pricking up her ears. Just because

they were long and silly now and got in the way,

it didn't mean she couldn't hear as well as ever.

You're always on guard when you're a dog.

Come to think of it, it would be useful really

to have three eyes.

•Best•

At last the day of the dog show
arrived. Harry had been dreading it,
but – just like all those things we
don't want to happen – it came
anyway. Poor Bonnie had been bathed
and brushed so much she was blinding
white – with, of course, a smart, dark blue
bow to keep the hair out of her eyes.

"Hello, Snowy Fox, how're you doing?"
whispered Harry as they sat on the sofa
while Mum got her bag of tricks ready.

"Three brushes, comb, toothbrush, toothpaste, wet wipes, eye-stain remover, cotton buds, change of collar and lead... Is that everything?"

"How about the washing machine in case she gets dirty?" muttered Harry, but Mum didn't hear.

She was so nervous. What would she do if Bonnie didn't even win a rosette? Harry couldn't bear to think about it.

But what if Bonnie actually won Best in Show, and then Mum *kept* going to dog shows? That was an even worse prospect.

Harry heaved a huge sigh, and Bonnie answered with a tiny one of her own.

The town hall was already buzzing with woofs and wags when they arrived. They asked the man at the door where they had to go. He squinted at Bonnie through the mesh of her smart dog carrier and smiled.

"From what I've seen so far, she might be the smallest dog in the show!"

"She'll be the best dog!" said Mum stoutly, and Harry cringed.

The show would take place in the main hall, where people were already sitting down to get a good view. Bonnie heard all the yaps and yips, and the occasional deep bark, and began to shiver.

"It's all right, Bons," Harry whispered. "This'll soon be over."

The man had told them to go round by the stage to the back area set aside for competitors. There they saw a long row of special cages, some of which already had dogs of all sizes sitting in them. A lady in a white jacket took Mum's name and checked her list. "So this is Bonnie. Your first show?"

Mum nodded nervously.

"Oh, you'll have a *lovely* time! Bonnie
is number twenty-three – see that kennel?
That's hers. There's water in there, and
a cushion. Just pop her in."

"I don't want her caged up like a prisoner,
Mum," Harry whispered.

The lady heard him. "Oh, she'll be *fine* –
all the dogs *love* it in their special hotels!"

How do *you* know? thought Harry,
but he said nothing.

Mum held open the kennel
door and Harry pushed the miserable
little dog inside. Her silky tail drooped. She
wouldn't look at them.

"Oh dear," said Mum, making the catch
firm. "But she'll be fine in a minute."

"Will she?" said Harry.

Just then the dog show official came over.
"Look," she said to Mum, "since this is your
first show, why not come along with me
for coffee?"

"Oh thanks, I'd like that," said Mum breathlessly. "Come on, Harry."

"I'm not leaving Bonnie on her own."

"Sorry, dear," said the lady, "but children under sixteen aren't allowed to stay back here without their parents. It's the rule. Come and have a cake."

Harry poked a finger through the mesh of kennel number 23 and tried to stroke Bonnie's nose. She wouldn't come closer.

"I know you're cross with us, Bonnie," he said softly. "I hate it too. But I'll be back soon – promise!"

Left alone, Bonnie pressed herself against the wire of her kennel cage to see if she could tell which way they had gone.

There were dogs each side of her and the sound of dogs in the distance, but all she wanted was her human pack.

She mooched around, then flopped down on the cushion with her nose on her paws. A Labrador went past with his owner, then a springer spaniel holding her head high.

Bonnie wanted to call out to the bigger
dogs, tell them to nudge the latch of her cage
with their noses so she could get out, but she
just gave one tiny yip then settled back.

It was no good. For about five minutes
she felt sad and alone. Of course she
knew Harry *wanted* to come back,
but what if he didn't? What if
her pack forgot her?

She stared at the barred door to the kennel, and realized something exciting. It didn't go all the way down to the floor, and there was quite a large gap in the corner. She padded over and investigated, testing the space with her nose. These kennels were designed for much bigger dogs. It would be a tight squeeze – it might even hurt a bit – but Bonnie was sure she could get out. She knew she'd have to be careful. If one of those people in white jackets saw her, she'd be straight back in that cage before you could say "Crufts".

Suddenly everything went quiet. Bonnie's sharp black eyes watched … and when there was no one around she pushed and wriggled and squeezed, holding her breath, front paws pulling, back paws scrabbling to push – and POP! She was through. She jumped down to the ground and raced off.

Hiding by the end kennel in the row,

Bonnie sniffed, trying to trace the trail of Harry and his mum, but there were so many scents of dogs and strange people that she could pick nothing up. Which way did they go?

She took a guess and trotted off, slipping up some stone steps and through a big old door. She was in a long wide corridor, shady and quiet. In the distance she heard a voice making announcements – and, for a second, thought it might be better to go back. They'd be bound to come soon.

She found herself outside a heavy polished
door standing ajar, with *Mayor's Parlour*
written on it in curly gold script. Somebody
was moving about inside. Bonnie stopped.
She thought it might be her pack, so she
poked her head round the door to see.

The room smelled of polish and leather, and sunlight fell across a table covered in green felt – gleaming on the silver cups lined up, ready to be presented to the winners of the dog show. But the trophies were disappearing into a large rucksack held by a pale-faced young man with a baseball cap pulled low over his eyes. He didn't notice Bonnie watching, but swung round to the cabinet where the mayor's chain and some other antique objects were displayed. *Smash!* went his hammer – and then those precious things vanished into his rucksack too.

Something about his scent told Bonnie
he was bad. She darted forward and took
hold of the leg of his jeans. *"Grrrrrrrr."*

"Gerroff, you little rat!" he hissed,
and kicked out.

Bonnie went flying back.
She didn't like that at all,
and set up
a terrific
yelping which
echoed all round
the big old room.
"Yip yip yip yip YIP!"
"Shut *up*! Shut it,
will you? Good dog.
Here, puppy!"

74

He bent and
held out a hand, but
Bonnie darted forward
and sank her needle-sharp
teeth into his fingers
making him stagger back in shock.
He swore at her, hoisted the rucksack
onto his shoulder and tried
to walk out of the room
as if nothing had
happened. But
Bonnie gave chase.
Feeling her snapping
at his heels, the man
quickened his pace until
he too broke into a run.

He turned a corner at the end of the corridor and blundered into a tea trolley laid ready for the mayor and his guests. *Crash!* The trolley went flying, along with its jug of milk, little pots of jam, honey and cream, plates of scones and sandwiches.

Mmm, cream, thought Bonnie, as most of it landed on her. She narrowly escaped being knocked out by the milk jug, but the little dog kept running.

The burglar was starting to panic. He ran on and reached the back door of the town hall, but as he stopped to open it Bonnie was at his ankles again.

"Grrrrr-rrrrr … *grrrrr*."

Outside, he grabbed a rubbish bin and overturned it to try to halt her chase. Dust, scraps of paper, soggy teabags and cigarette ends all rained down on Bonnie's head – but she was so angry that she didn't notice. She kept running.

As she raced after him across the quiet back lawn, three familiar figures rounded the corner on their way to the dog show – and stopped still in amazement.

"Is that … is that … *Bonnie*?" whispered Olga to Zack and Zena as the little dog hurtled past.

Zack looked at Zena; Zena looked at Zack; and before Olga could protest, they were off across the lawn after Bonnie,

who was off across the lawn after the
burglar, who just at that moment ran
straight into the burly chest of the security
guard at the rear gate. Tripped up by
Bonnie, the robber crashed to the ground
and a silver cup rolled slowly out of his
rucksack to land at the guard's feet.

"What we got here then?" said the
security guard. "Looks like you've
been rumbled, mate."

"*Yip Yip Yip!*" barked Bonnie, just
as Zack and Zena caught up.

"Wow!
Super-Wabbit
strikes again,"
panted Zack.

"YIP!" said Bonnie.
She jumped up onto
the burglar's stomach
and shook out
her filthy fur
in triumph.

Meanwhile Harry and
his mum had returned
to find kennel number
23 empty. They
couldn't believe it,
because the door was still shut.
They ran to find an official, and found
themselves back in the main hall, where
everyone was now gathered, waiting for the
first competitors to come in.

"Somebody's stolen our dog!" Mum
gasped to a man with
a clipboard.
"What?"

"They must've taken her out of the kennel!" Harry puffed. He felt sick.

"What kind of dog?"

"Our beautiful Maltese," wailed Mum. "She's tiny, white and … perfect."

They didn't notice that something was going on near the stage. People were whispering, and pacing to and fro, and then the mayor and some other important-looking people walked up the steps to make an announcement.

"Ladies and gentlemen – and dogs! – may we have your attention. Something most unusual has just happened. A burglar has been caught stealing the dog show trophies and other valuables, as well as the priceless chain that has been worn by every mayor of this town for the past two hundred years!"

The audience gasped.

The mayor went on. "And it's very fitting that the heroine of the hour is … a dog! Does anybody here own this little lady?"

84

Harry and his mum gaped. Trotting up the steps onto the stage, on a lead held by the security guard, was a small white dog they recognized. Only she wasn't very white. Nor was she fit for a show any more. She was filthy, streaked with dirt, jam and honey, dripping with milk, and covered in cigarette ends and scraps of paper. The blue bow had slipped down over one eye, and a squashed cream scone was stuck on her head.

Harry didn't wait for Mum.
He raced toward the stage,
up the steps, and swept
Bonnie up in a huge hug.
She wriggled with delight
and licked his face all over, and
everybody clapped. Mum followed him,
and found herself shaking the mayor's hand.

Two press photographers clicked away.

"You've got a very special little dog here,"
said the mayor. "Can I assume she was
due to take part in the show?"

Harry's mum nodded ruefully.

"Well, never mind. She's done something
much more important today. She doesn't
need a trophy, but we'll make sure
you get a special rosette –

because there's no doubt in anybody's mind
that this little Maltese is—"

Harry didn't let him finish.

"BEST IN SHOW!" he shouted –
and Zack and Zena and Olga and everybody
in the audience cheered like mad.

BONNIE yawned. What a long day!
So much fuss about that silly man and
all the silver stuff. And back home Mum had
bathed her, then taken her sharp scissors
and trimmed her coat all over.

"No more shows,"
Mum had said to Harry. "I mean, how
could she do any better than that?"
Harry had winked at Bonnie.
He'd never looked happier.

Bonnie licked her lips, remembering
the chicken and gravy for tea, and nobody
fussing when her ears dipped in the bowl.
Tomorrow they'd play in the sandpit next door,
and life would be back to normal. There'd be
walks in the park, and special treats when
she stayed where she was told, and she'd make
Harry laugh by chasing him around the room...

Yes, she thought.
The best thing about being a dog
is knowing you're needed.

Love Bonnie? Then why
not read all six of her
tail-wagging adventures!

To find out more about the books
and the real-life Bonnie who inspired
them, visit belmooney.co.uk

A Day in the Life of the Real Bonnie

Bonnie says:

I wake up on Bel's bed, usually jammed up against Robin because I always try to push him out. It's not that I don't love him, 'cos I do, it's just that the bed is only big enough for two. I don't know why Robin doesn't realize he should be in a basket on the landing!

The two of them stumble about, yawning, having a shower, getting dressed and all those boring things. They must be envious of my simple but stylish white fur coat (it's always in fashion). Downstairs for breakfast, and I have my "Find the Biscuits" game on the window

seat. Robin hides biscuits (well,
actually it's crunchy tooth-
cleaning solid food) and treats
among the cushions then lifts me up there to
hunt for them. I sniff out the yummy treats
first, then go back for the healthy stuff (a bit
like you with your peas, I expect).

A drink of water, and then I'm ready for
the day. When the rest of the pack has
finished eating and reading the
newspapers, that is.

My normal day isn't very exciting. Bel
works in one room and Robin works in
another – and I have a bed by each of their
desks. What to do? Divide my time of course,
so one of them won't be hurt. But I suppose I
spend most time on the blue bed under Bel's
desk, because I have to give her ideas for her

books, you see. I'm really not sure how she'd manage without me.

After lunch, Bel and Robin put on my harness (and one of my coats if it's winter – this should always match my collar, of course. A dog-about-town can't be too careful with her appearance) and take me for a walk. I like going through the allotments where there are lots of strange smells. At lampposts and on walls I pick up interesting p-mails from other dogs. That's how we network, you see.

Sometimes Bel will go to read in the conservatory in the afternoon and usually fall asleep because it's sunny and warm. I like that, because we snuggle up in a puppy-pile, like I dimly remember from when I was born.

About five thirty it's supper-time! Robin feeds me – a mixture of meat and biscuits, but I sometimes pretend I'm not hungry, just to annoy him and Bel. They don't have their own supper until about eight, and I always drag my basket over to the table, so I can keep an eye on them (you know, make sure they're behaving themselves). After that I like it best if they're in the sitting-room, on the same sofa with me in between them. Maybe they read, maybe they watch TV – but what matters is that the pack is all together, warm and cosy until bedtime, and then all through the night.

Bel Mooney is a well-known journalist and author of many books for adults and children, including the hugely popular Kitty series. She lives in Bath with her husband and real-life Maltese dog, Bonnie, who is the inspiration for this series. Bel says of the real Bonnie: "She makes me laugh and transforms my life with her intelligence, courage and affection. And I just know she's going to pick out a really good card for my birthday."

Find out more about Bel at belmooney.co.uk

Sarah McMenemy is a highly respected artist who illustrates for magazines and newspapers and has worked on diverse commissions all over the world, including art for the London Underground, CD covers and stationery. She illustrated the bestselling City Skylines series and is the creator of the picture books *Waggle* and *Jack's New Boat*.
She lives in London.

Find out more about Sarah at
sarahmcmenemy.com